I0526945

Paula Garcia Taveras is a new author focusing on helping children learn to make friends with God through a colorful, and an imagery story such as Phoenix the Brave Bird. Paula's literary background started when a local newspaper in her native country, *the D.R.,* announced a children's literary contest, 'The Lion King' and she participated in the third category. She is also a member of the Society of Children's Book Writers and Illustrators. Paula lives in Cherry Hill, NJ with her son, Alejandro, and plans to write more books to help today's youth grow up with strong compassionate values.

i

Phoenix
the Brave Bird

Paula Garcia Taveras

AUSTIN MACAULEY PUBLISHERS™

LONDON • CAMBRIDGE • NEW YORK • SHARJAH

Copyright © Paula Garcia Taveras (2018)

Ordering Information:
Quantity sales: special discounts are available on quantity purchases by corporations, associations, and others. For details, contact the publisher at the address below.

Taveras, Paula Garcia.
Phoenix the Brave Bird

ISBN 9781643780986 (Paperback)
ISBN 9781643780993 (Hardback)
ISBN 9781643781006 (E-Book)

The main category of the book — JUVENILE FICTION / Short Stories
www.austinmacauley.com/us

First Published (2018)
Austin Macauley Publishers LLC
40 Wall Street, 28th Floor
New York, NY 10005
USA

mail-usa@austinmacauley.com
+1 (646) 5125767

With all my heart to these two little princesses: J.J.C. whom when I met her, barely was four and a half years old and even though I shared a brief period of time with her, it was enough to captivate me with her spark and joy. Today, she probably does not remember me anymore but I do remember her every single day…

And in honor of my lovely niece, Karla.

First at all, I thank to my Lord and Savior, Jesus Christ because everything is by him and for him. Secondly, this project could not really succeed without the contribution of more than one hand, therefore, I appreciate the help of those who have made possible the presentation of this book: Mr. Fernando Méndez, Oscar Rivera, Mrs. Soonhwa Wiesner, and Lee Ann. I thank to my son, Alejandro for giving me ideas when I was in doubt, and to all friends and people that in one way supported the project.

Once upon a time, there was a bird named Phoenix who lived in the woods in the middle of nowhere. It would be difficult to find anything more beautiful than Phoenix.

His intensely golden body was covered with scarlet-red feathers, and his eyes were like two bright lights that lit the darkness.

The soft sound of his singing made even the most restless beast feel as calm as could be.

Every morning before the sun came out, he woke up early, rushing to shout: "Woo hoo, Sun, I beat you one more time!"

He'd stretch out his long wings and start to fly around the woods, still moist from the dew of the night. Then, he would dive into the

sea—splash!

And in a few seconds, his body was clean.

"Brrrr!!!" He was shivering because of the cold while he shook the water from his feathers.

"Now it is time for my delicious breakfast. Yummy in my tummy!" he said as he started to fly.

He sat on some branches and with his beak, oh, the fruits he would try.

10

And that was the way he spent his day, until the night came to say,
"Hey, go and get some rest."

Phoenix had a selfless nature. He liked to defend the other animals also living there.

One day during his usual routine, he heard a desperate voice cry out: "Help, help, I need help, please!"

Phoenix flew over to where the voice was and found a multi-colored hummingbird trying to not be the lunch of a hungry crow.

"Don't hurt him!" Phoenix demanded.

"And why are you sticking your beak in?" asked the crow, sounding very mean.

The crow cornered the hummingbird, and a sad end looked impossible to prevent.

Phoenix decided to act. Using his strength, he pushed the crow away from the hummingbird.

The crow ended up lying on the ground and Phoenix, stuck between two branches of a tree, could not get free.

Then the crow was angry, and in a threatening voice said, "I will pluck out your eyes, and no more will you see!"

"Oh no!!"

When the poor hummingbird heard this, his little heart fell, for he believed he was the cause of all that befell.

Phoenix plucked up his courage and his body transformed into fire. The crow became so filled with fright that all he could do was quickly take flight.

Then, Phoenix returned to its natural form. The hummingbird came closer to him and began to peck the branches of the

tree—Tic, tic, tic!!

And Phoenix finally got released.

"Thanks for saving me. My name is Tonino," said the hummingbird.

"My name is Phoenix."

"You are very brave. Do you mind if I call you Phoenix the Brave Bird?"

"Phoenix the Brave Bird? Ha! I like it!" he answered with a glowing smile.

"By the way, this is the first time I have seen you around."

"I am passing through, and am actually headed to..."

"Welcome to the woods! If you want, you can stay," Phoenix interrupted him.

"The truth is..." he hesitated trying to make his mind.

"Well!! I do believe I will accept, but only for a few days."

The two smiled at each other and at that very moment, a beautiful friendship was born.

Now Phoenix had someone to play with. They had flying races, they swam in the sea, and they even rode on the dolphins as if they were surfing.

17

Life was happy, but their happiness awoke the forces of evil and jealousy, making the cunning fox show up and immediately manipulate the circumstances. He set to work.

On one of their fun-filled afternoons, Tonino suddenly stopped in a weird mood.

"Are you all right?" Phoenix asked.

"Shhh! Listen, I think it has arrived."

"Who or what?" asked Phoenix.

"The wind. Remember I told you I would be here for just a while?"

"Yes, I remember."

"The reason is my expedition. In the Great Himalaya Mountains, on a merry-go-round, I will slide down. Yee haw!! In the Amazonian Jungle, to the rhythm of the samba, my body will dance. Tun, tu tu tu, tun tun!! Along with the penguins, on the ice of the Antarctic, we'll race and skate. Brrrr!! And finally, on the beaches of the Caribbean, the sun will touch my face."

"Wow! It sounds like an exciting adventure!" Phoenix said.

"Yes! And you will come with me, right? You are my best friend, and we will be together until the end."

The invitation was a surprise for Phoenix who, nevertheless, very excitedly said, "Count on me!"

"The wind! The wind, Phoenix! It is blowing our way now and it will carry us faster to the expedition. Hurry up!"

And the cunning fox, had found the perfect timing to give his poison to the two.

He quickly went to Phoenix and asked him, "Are you really so brave?"

"Yes, Sir Fox, indeed I am," he responded with conviction.

The fox gave him a sinister look and used his wiles to make him stumble.

20

"Have you thought about all the dangers you will find? And besides, these beautiful woods you may never inhabit again in your life?"

And for the first time, Phoenix doubted, and when fear knocked: Toc, toc!

The access he allowed, because the woods were all he had known since he was born.

"Phoenix, please do not be swayed!" Tonino cried.

Phoenix ran away. He wanted to be alone and try to understand.

Tonino felt disappointed, for he believed that his special friend had failed him.

The evil plan of the cunning fox worked, but still, he reserved for Tonino the final thrust.

22

He approached him silently and blew a spell right into his face:

Fuuuuuuu!!!

In just seconds, Tonino's disappointment changed to hatred, and then, he was sent down the path of bitterness.

Phoenix, his emotions to calm, thought of his great deeds, and to his courage gave balm.

"I will always be brave," said he.

He returned to find his friend, very cheerful and convinced that the expedition would succeed.

"Hey, Tonino, here I am!"

23

And Tonino, with harsh words, answered him thus: "For what? The chance has been taken from us. Go away. With you, I do not want to play."

Phoenix did not believe what he heard, and left very hurt.

The mission of the cunning fox was totally done. Proud and triumphant, he started humming a song:

"La-la-la, clac, clac, la-la-la!"

And to create new discord, to other places he explored.

The days went by; for Tonino's forgiveness, Phoenix kept asking.

He took him flowers and all kinds of gifts, but despite his efforts, continued the rift.

"Leave me alone! You will not change my mind with your tricks!"

Tonino met new friends and his love for
Phoenix came to an end.

Phoenix felt alone. He cried all day long, and
he refused to eat.

The woods, which possessed eyes and ears,
did not ignore the sadness of Phoenix and
wishing to help him, it turned itself into
an old owl.

"Little creature, what is the reason for your
affliction?" the owl asked him.

And Phoenix, his story, told.

With wise words the old owl responded,
"When we have used up all our resources
and nothing is achieved, in the help of God
we need to believe."

"God? Who is God? And where can I find
him?" Phoenix asked with hope.

"God is everywhere, and can be much closer
than you can perceive."

The old owl began to move his wings, which
sounded like a strong turbine: "Fu, fu, fu!"

And he disappeared into the sky.

Phoenix was confused, but at once
began to search.

He climbed mountains and dove into the sea,
but nowhere God could he see.

It soon grew dark, and already exhausted he
settled down, lodging under a tree.

"Where are you, God?" he asked. Breathless
and overcome by slumber, he fell asleep.

He dreamt his heart had a door, and that
door opened, revealing a beautiful rainbow.
Its colors were so bright that it blocked the
light from Phoenix's eyes, but he could still
see the cloud approaching him slowly.

The presence of the cloud filled him with great peace and, with relief, he exclaimed: "God, here you are!"

"Just pray," he heard the cloud say.

"Pray? What is pray? And with that, will you help?" he replied.

"It is to ask for something and to believe with all your might that your wish you will receive."

Phoenix woke up, and then understood that God lived in his heart.

With his two little legs bent, to the floor he went. His prayer was a sublime melody that everyone in the woods got stuck in.

But what it was meant to be, Phoenix could not predict. In fact, nothing happened that day, neither the next.

He thought God lied to him, and crestfallen, murmured, "God, praying to you did not work."

He cried with deep feeling. From his eyes, two pearly drops fell to the ground and caused an effect: where in nature only drought had been, was once again filled with green.

And there Tonino appeared, asking with tears, "Can you forgive your best friend?"

Phoenix jumped for joy and welcomed him with a hug.

"Thank you, God!" Phoenix exclaimed.

"God? Who is God?" Tonino asked.

"It is a long story that

I will share on our way."

And the perfect wind blew the two to their fabulous expedition.

THE END

34

Illustrated book for children

between ages 7 and 12.

36